For Eddie, Lewis, Hayley, Jake and Kate – A.H.
For Linda Lyall – M.M.

First published in Great Britain in 1987
This revised edition published 2015
Deepdene Lodge, Deepdene Avenue,
Dorking, Surrey, RH5 4AT, UK
www.bonnierpublishing.com

Text copyright © Anita Harper, 1987, 2007
Illustrations copyright © Mary McQuillan, 2007

Printed and bound in China

ISBN: 978 1 84812 504 9 (paperback)

1 3 5 7 9 10 8 6 4 2

It's Not Fair!

By Anita Harper
Illustrated by Mary McQuillan

Piccadilly Press • London

When Mum and Dad brought my baby brother home, everyone fussed over him.

It wasn't fair!

"What about me?"

"You're a big girl now," my mum said.

I'm not THAT big.

People are always doing things for HIM.
I have to do things for myself.

It's not fair!

If he makes a mess, it's all right.

If I make a mess, I get into trouble.

That's not fair!

When we go out, I have to walk.
But my baby brother can ride.

It makes me MAD!

When the babysitter is here,
and my brother screams,
she tries to find out what's wrong.

When I scream

she tells me to be quiet.

It's not fair!

Now my brother's getting bigger.

The other day, we went for a walk
in the rain. He wanted to walk,
but my mum wouldn't let him.

He didn't think
that was fair!

And when we go to the park he wants to slide down the hill, but HE isn't big enough.

He doesn't think
THAT'S fair either!

When **I** go to playgroup,
my brother wants to go too,
but he can't.

He doesn't think
THAT'S fair at all.

Now, when my friends come over,
my brother wants to play with us,

but he's too small.

He lets us know he doesn't think that's fair.

Sometimes **I'm** allowed to stay up late,
but my brother has to go to bed.

He screams and screams, because
it's not fair!

My brother has started to talk now.
Today I'm going to a party
and he can't go.

Do you know what he said?

"It's not fair!"